BASKETBALL

**THOMAS S. OWENS
DIANA STAR HELMER**

TWENTY-FIRST CENTURY BOOKS
BROOKFIELD, CONNECTICUT

To Jack Twyman and Rick Barry, two of basketball's best friends. And to Darlene and Dick Tomhave, two of our best friends.

Designed by Molly Heron

Cover photograph courtesy of NBA Photos (© Jennifer Pottheiser)

Photographs courtesy of NBA Photos: pp. 7 (both © Andrew D. Bernstein), 8 (© Andrew D. Bernstein), 10 (© Andrew D. Bernstein), 17 (© Glenn James), 21 (© Wen Roberts), 27 (© Jim Cummins), 39 (© Scott Cunningham), 40, 45 (© Andrew D. Bernstein), 54 (© Garrett Ellwood); AP/Wide World Photos: pp. 14, 15, 29, 52; UPI/Corbis-Bettmann: pp. 23, 47; SportsChrome-USA: pp. 32 (© Rich Kane), 34 (© Rich Kane); Reuters/Archive Photos: pp. 36 (© Sue Ogrocki), 49 (© Mike Blake)

Owens, Thomas S., 1960-
    Basketball / by Thomas S. Owens and Diana Star Helmer.
    p.   cm.— (Game Plan)
    Includes bibliographical references and index.
    Summary: Describes how professional men's basketball teams prepare for games, analyze the games afterwards for improvement, develop strategies, and build themselves through player selection.
    ISBN 0-7613-3234-0 (lib. bdg.)
    1. Basketball—United States—Juvenile literature. [1. Basketball.]
I. Helmer, Diana Star, 1962- . II. Title. III. Series: Owens, Tom, 1960- Game Plan.
GV885.1.O84   1999
796.323'0973—dc21   98-35530   CIP
                                                                         AC

Published by Twenty-First Century Books
A Division of The Millbrook Press, Inc.
2 Old New Milford Road
Brookfield, Connecticut 06804

Copyright © 1999 by Thomas S. Owens and Diana Star Helmer
All rights reserved.
Printed in the United States of America
1 3 5 4 2

Contents

1. **Magic in the air** 5
2. **The brains behind the game** 12
3. **In the middle** 20
4. **Going forward** 26
5. **On guard** 32
6. **Off the bench** 38
7. **Basketball basics** 43
8. **Devastating duos** 48

   Glossary 56
   For more information 61
   Index 63

MAGIC IN THE AIR

In 1991 *Sports Illustrated* called the NBA Finals "The Magic and Michael Show." To fans across the United States, that's just what those TV games were.

It was the first time superstar Michael Jordan had played in the Finals. Jordan, all by himself, had made the Chicago Bulls famous since joining them six years before. There never had been a player like Mike. Who else could leap away from opponents, away from the basket and hang in midair, faking side to side until blockers were baffled and he had a clean shot? They called him "Air" because that's where he spent so much of his time.

But it was Earvin Johnson that fans called "Magic."

Magic had been with the Los Angeles Lakers since 1979. Two years later, he had signed the biggest sports contract ever at that time: a 25-year deal worth $25 million. "Magic will make the impossible shot at the buzzer appear routine," the Chicago *Tribune* reported. But that was not why he was worth so much to the team.

"If you are open, Magic will get you the ball," the *Tribune* continued. "He may not be looking your way, but that is no problem. He will throw the ball over his shoulder or between his legs while he is running full speed in the other direction. And the next thing you know, you are making an uncontested ten-foot jumper or stuffing the ball through the basket."

A Magic Team

Johnson did more than score points. He led his team, held them together, helped them work together to score—and something more. When Magic missed some games due to injury, L.A. coach Paul Westhead said that without his star guard the Lakers' games were "neat, clean, minimal talking, no nonsense. But when Magic returned, it was like Looney Tunes. He created havoc. Everybody started laughing again. It was unreal."

It was Magic.

Michael Jordan wasn't always so easy to like. Jordan loved the game as much as Magic. Sometimes, Jordan seemed to walk on air, carried by the wish to sink a basket. He could make shots from places on the floor that even surprised himself. And after he did, Jordan might just be so happy he'd dance for the opposing team's bench. That's how Jordan told it. Opponents said he seemed like a bad sport, a show-off.

His own team didn't always know what to think. Jordan could sure play like no one else. Problem was, no one else got a chance to try. Jordan's drive often left his teammates empty-handed. Reporters called talented players like Scottie Pippen, John Paxson, Horace Grant, and veteran Bill Cartwright "The Jordanaries"—it rhymed with "ordinary."

The Bulls were unhappy. But no matter how unhappy they were, the team couldn't fire its biggest star. The only thing left was to keep changing coaches until someone figured out a way to win with Michael. The 1991 Bulls were trying their fourth different coach in six seasons.

A Ball for All

Coach Phil Jackson told *Sports Illustrated* that when he joined the Bulls in 1989, his game plan was to "incorporate all five players"—which, he admitted, "was a difficult sell to Michael." Jackson explained to the Chicago *Tribune*, "We told him, maybe guys are not as talented as you'd like them to be, but this is as good as we can get under the present situation."

Superstars in action in Game 5 of the 1991 NBA Finals: Chicago Bulls Michael Jordan (left) and Los Angeles Lakers Magic Johnson

Jackson's plan for more equality wasn't easy for the rest of the team, either. Jackson tried "to treat Michael as equally as possible on the court," but he admitted "there is a difference in the way he's treated [because] there's a difference in the way he produces—a big difference. And that must be weighed." That resulted in "jealousies that other players must overcome," Jackson said.

What happens before a game is part of the game, too.

Jackson decided that part of training and practicing would be reading, so team members had things to talk about and think about together. Jackson put film clips from movies like *The Wizard of Oz* into practice films to show there was more to basketball than shooting; there was "brains" and "courage" and "heart." Sometimes, Jackson would put the team on a bus instead of a plane so they could relax and see the beautiful countryside together.

During Jackson's second season at the helm, *Sports Illustrated* wrote that "for the first time since Jordan came into the league in 1984, the Bulls [have] gotten away from the 'one-man team' label." And, for the first time in its 25-year history, the Chicago Bulls' team was going to the NBA Finals!

They got there by playing as a team. But in the first game of the Finals, at home in Chicago, it was the Magic and Michael Show, and Jordan was the

Chicago Bulls coach Phil Jackson at the 1991 NBA Finals. A coach plays an important role in developing game strategy and must be flexible enough to change strategy mid-game if the plan isn't working.

star. He jumped, he soared, he scored 36 points, leaving other Bulls in the dust with an average of just 6 points apiece. Jordan guarded Magic, holding him to 6 points in the first half. But Magic simply passed to teammates who were open. The Bulls double-teamed him. But they couldn't stop Magic from directing his team, and L.A. beat the Bulls—beat them in Chicago—in a thrilling 93–91 match.

"It almost lived up to the hype," Magic grinned.

And the predictions. This was the ninth time Magic had led his Lakers to the Finals. They'd won it all four times before. Five key L.A. players had a history in the Finals. Not one Bull had a single game's experience in the championship series until now.

> **Famed Chicago Bulls coach Phil Jackson played in the NBA for 13 years. At 6 foot 8, Jackson had long legs and arms. How long? As a teen, he could sit in the back seat of a car and open both doors at once—one door handle in each hand.**

And "now" was something Jackson, Jordan, and the Bulls could change. In Game 2, Scottie Pippen guarded Magic Johnson. Jordan followed Jackson's game plan by leading the Bulls' offense, instead of trying to do it all himself. John Paxson scored 16 points, one of five Bulls who scored in double digits. This time Jordan's Bulls shared the game, shared a win, a sweet win at home, 107–86, tying the series.

Chicago's Team Effort

The teams played Game 3 in L.A., struggling neck and neck right into overtime. Chicago's Pippen stayed with Magic, but now the Lakers were double-teaming Jordan. They kept him from the basket, and by the third quarter, L.A. was up by 13 points. Coach Jackson started rotating his players. In eight minutes, eight different Chicago Bulls scored—with not one point from Jordan. But it was Jordan's last-second jumper that tied the game into overtime, and Jordan's steal—and assist—that proved he could both lead a winning team and be a team player.

By Game 4, two key L.A. players were hurt. Those who went the distance—Magic Johnson and Sam Perkins—were post-up players.

Scottie Pippen was high-point scorer for Game 5 of the 1991 NBA Finals. His great effort led the Chicago Bulls to victory over the L.A. Lakers.

They liked to keep their backs to the basket, turn away from the player guarding them, and shoot around him. The Bulls' game plan added double-teaming for L.A.'s post-up players: No matter where the Lakers turned, there was somebody blocking the shot. By the time L.A. could pass, the shot clock was almost ready to blow. The Bulls won, 97–82. They were ahead in the series, three games to one. But there was one more game in L.A.

The score—108–101—tells it all: Game 5 was tight. But the Lakers needed something they couldn't get: their injured players. Chicago needed a team effort, and got it. For the first time in the Finals, a Bull other than Jordan—Scottie Pippen— scored the most points for the team.

The Magic and Michael show was over. Each of the stars had lived up to his fans' expectations, leading his team in scoring, assists, and minutes played. But what happens after a game is part of the game, too.

Down in the locker room, the Bulls knelt together and said the Lord's Prayer. Then, as Chicago players and coaches gave interviews and laughed and celebrated with families and friends, Michael Jordan sat on a bench and cried.

"I never showed this kind of emotion before in public," he said, his voice cracking.

Coming into Chicago's locker room to offer congratulations, Magic Johnson told reporters, "I know exactly what Michael is feeling now because I felt that way later in my career, when it took so much more effort and sweat to win it.

"It's going to taste sweet for them."

Not all pro players become rich. Many players in basketball's first-ever card set, made in 1948 by Bowman Chewing Gum, were never paid a cent. The brand-new NBA and its players seemed happy enough to get free attention from trading cards.

2 THE BRAINS BEHIND THE GAMES

A player's statistics and his team's record can usually convince fans that an athlete has talent—whether or not fans agree on just how great that player is.

Judging off-the-court leaders—the head coaches and general managers—isn't always as easy. If a team is losing, does that mean the coach's game plan doesn't work, or that his players need more time to fine-tune the strategy? What types of people make the best coaches and managers? Where do these people learn to judge talent and create winning game plans?

Bulls' general manager Jerry Krause was credited with putting all the pieces in place for Chicago's 1990s "dynasty." He acquired every player for the Bulls' first championship team except for superstar Michael Jordan. Krause's eye for hardwood talent made it easy to assume he had been around the game all his life, perhaps as a player or coach.

Yet Krause landed his job with the Bulls after scouting for baseball's Chicago White Sox. That's because Bulls' owner Jerry Reinsdorf also owned the White Sox, and he knew Krause could assemble players into winning combinations. Of course, Krause knew basketball, too. For more than a decade, he worked as a scout for NBA teams such as the Suns and the Lakers.

The Homework Never Ends

Studying players—your own, and others—is the role of team builders. Many teams have a video coordinator. One person is in charge of filming practices and games. In what becomes all-night work, the video coordinator will edit special tapes. Some tapes will show only defensive plays. Others may focus on the work of one player. The morning after a game, the team can see its success, or failure—again and again! The video coordinator also will help find tapes of upcoming opponents. The tapes could even be peeked at between halves in a game.

> Who's the best shooter? Anyone who "hangs the net," making the ball sail so cleanly through the hoop that the netting boomerangs back and gets tangled around the rim.

Not unlike plain fans, coaching staffs use common sources of information: television, newspapers, and the Internet. A common question about future foes is: Who is injured or playing hurt? A player with an aching back may not be as threatening on jump shots as usual. Sometimes, the simplest information is the most helpful. Chicago's Toni Kukoc gets more layups against teams who forget that he's left-handed. Teams that make him shoot at the right side of the hoop, using his weaker hand, do better defensively.

Teams use computers to study their own and other teams' statistics. Coaches can learn about other coaches and players. When a team is behind in the last 30 seconds, what kind of play do they choose the most? What type of shot does a star player like most, and from what spot on the court? Add up the numbers from the past, and a coach might predict the future. Knowing how to turn information into wins is the mark of a great coach.

Great coaches can start just about anywhere. Chuck Daly's first job coaching came at Punxsutawney High School in Pennsylvania, where he worked eight years. He spent another eight years in the college coaching ranks. Next, Daly was an assistant coach and mentor for former star player Billy Cunningham, when Cunningham took charge of the Philadelphia 76ers in 1977. All this led to Daly gaining leadership of his own NBA teams, earning more than 500 victories, taking Detroit to NBA titles in 1989 and 1990, as well as guiding the USA Dream Team to a gold medal in the 1992 Olympics.

Coach Chuck Daly guided the USA Dream Team to a gold medal in the 1992 Summer Olympics.

Records Break, Examples Don't

Arnold "Red" Auerbach was elected to the Basketball Hall of Fame in 1968. Auerbach led the Boston Celtics to nine NBA titles in 10 years. From 1959 to 1966, the Celtics won eight championships in a row. Auerbach is credited with 938 wins (1,037 counting post-season games). The NBA's Coach of the Year trophy is named after him. All this from a former college coach who never played a day in the NBA.

The legacy of Auerbach's game plan is not limited to his wins. Ten of his former players went on to coach NBA teams, too. "First and foremost, I considered myself a teacher," Auerbach said. "I taught basketball. If you were a Celtic, you learned to motivate and communicate."

Auerbach stepped down from coaching after the 1966 campaign, even though he continued as Boston's general manager. He was succeeded by the star he'd taught for so long, center Bill Russell. Russell was the Celtics' "player-coach" for three Celtic seasons. Doing both jobs, Russell

> "We were not as sophisticated as they are today (using VCRs, film, etc.) but between exhibition games and playoffs and regular season, we saw a lot of our opponents and knew pretty much what to do both as individuals and as a team."
>
> — Hall of Famer Jack Twyman, who played 1955–66, on how past teams scouted each other.

Boston Celtics Coach "Red" Auerbach (right) and Bill Russell in 1966 enjoying the Celtics' eighth straight NBA championship

led his teams to championship trophies in 1968 and 1969. And even after hanging up his sneakers, Russell kept doing double duty. He served as general manager and head coach in both Seattle and Sacramento.

When Russell took the coach's post, skeptics warned that scoring baskets may not teach a person how to lead others. Former player and TV announcer Pat Riley learned this was true when he became the Los Angeles Lakers' head coach in 1981.

"When I got the job, I wasn't ready and I knew it," he confessed to reporters. "I didn't have a philosophy, so I had to dive in, work as hard as I could, do all the research that I could and develop a philosophy."

Another Way to Fly

Boston great Larry Bird hadn't been near a team's bench since his 1992 retirement from the Celtics. Some Indiana fans may have thought it was a stunt to sell tickets when Bird, a native of French Lick, Indiana, was hired to coach his home state's Pacers in 1997. But time away from the game seemed to have given the famous player a chance to develop his philosophy, his own game plan.

> **Former Bulls coach Dick Motta had a temper. In one 1970s game, he yelled at the referees. Still angry, Motta kicked the basketball into the balcony. The refs never saw his drop-kicking tantrum. But the other coach got the technical foul for yelling too much about Motta's behavior.**

Bird's coaching brought the Pacers from a losing record to a play-off spot in his first season. The NBA named Bird Coach of the Year in his rookie season, only the fourth rookie coach ever to get the honor. Bird's Pacers were 58–24, the best record in the team's NBA history. (The season before Bird, Indiana's record was 39–43.) "He's absolutely the coach of the year," Pacers' point guard Mark Jackson told USA TODAY. "I think it's a no-brainer, because he's allowed us to be ourselves."

Bird encouraged his staff to "be themselves," too. He put Indiana's assistant coach, Dick Harter, in charge of the defense. Harter said the new coach had a trio of strengths. "Number one, he has a great feel and vision of the game. He sees everything that's happening, like a bird hovering over everything," Harter said. "Two, he's very honest in telling and correcting mistakes. Three, he's had a great amount of patience and composure during games. We've been in many close games, and I think his confidence in our players and system and that things are going to work out has been a great calming influence."

Larry Bird, who as an outstanding player for the Boston Celtics won three NBA titles, three MVP awards, and an Olympic gold medal, was inducted into the Basketball Hall of Fame in October 1998. He retired as a player in 1992, but later went on to a second successful career as coach of the Indiana Pacers. Here he makes a point to his coaching staff during a game.

Even nonfans knew about the strengths of Bird's coaching, thanks to national newspaper advice columnist Ann Landers. When Bird left some of his own players behind during a road trip because they didn't get to the airport on time, she praised the new coach for setting and sticking to the same rules for everyone involved.

A Hoop Is a Circle That Never Ends

The philosophy of coach Phil Jackson is talked and written about a lot, too. Jackson coached the Chicago Bulls to six championships in eight years. When his autobiography was published in 1996, he called it *Sacred Hoops*. Jackson's beliefs about basketball balance some Native American beliefs with Zen Buddhist ideas and others, searching for unity among players on the team.

Jackson didn't take the route of most former players who become coaches. After a successful playing career, Jackson learned the coaching trade in the Continental Basketball Association, a development/training league for the NBA, much like baseball's minor leagues.

When Jackson jumped from Bulls' assistant to head coach in 1989, he kept former college coach Fred "Tex" Winter at his side as an offensive coordinator. Winter is known as the father of the "triple post" offense, also called the "triangle," the game plan that fueled the Bulls to six championships.

Winter, who was 75 and still active as an assistant when the Bulls entered the 1997–98 postseason, was seen as an old face with an old idea by some skeptics. After all, his offensive game plan had been public since 1962, when he wrote a 226-page book. However, Jackson knew that rival teams ganged up on leading scorer Jordan. Even worse, Jackson worried that some Bulls' players were standing still, waiting for Jordan to do it all.

Winter's plan could divide scoring chances among all players, while taking some defensive pressure off "MJ." Winter stayed devoted to the game plan, because he says it is built on the seven rules of good offensive basketball:

1. Penetration
2. Spacing players 15-20 feet apart, but near the basket
3. The ball and players keep moving
4. All shots are followed by good rebounding position
5. The system uses all five players, with choices to pass to any of four teammates
6. The system responds to defensive moves
7. The system uses the talent of each player

No coach would argue with those goals, although coaches—and fans—argue about whether the "triangle" is the best way to achieve those goals. But the secret is more than the plan. The secret is the people—the team—putting any game plan into action.

3 IN THE MIDDLE

In basketball's early days, the tallest person on a team played center. Height came in handy for tip-offs and rebounds. Jumping ability helped, of course, but centers with long arms and legs might never need to leave their feet. Many never did leave their feet, simply because they didn't have athletic ability to go with their size.

Centers of old were shooting machines, no matter what. They were often known as ballhogs. If they got the "rock," the ball was headed for the basket. Even worse, some centers who held the ball were like ticking bombs. Centers hired just for their size might pass poorly and dribble worse. Such a center faced with two defenders would be ripe for a turnover.

Glasses-wearing George Mikan was the NBA's first starring center with the 1950s Minneapolis Lakers, leading the league in scoring three times during his career. But it was 6-foot-10 Bill Russell of the Boston Celtics who rewrote the book on what a center could achieve. "Players just didn't block shots until Russell came into the league," Boston coach Red Auerbach said.

Many of Russell's blocked shots seem nothing like today's rejections, where a center will swat a foe's shot out of bounds and into the seats. Russell would bat down the ball, take control, then pass to a teammate. In fact, Russell might have been credited with a blocked shot and steal on the same play.

Though Russell had signed for a then-huge $17,000, the Boston media questioned his future. First off, he was skinny. Next, playing in the 1956 Olympics caused Russell to miss the first 24 games of the season. Worst of all, he wasn't scoring tons of points. But how Russell scored, when he scored, changed the game, too: Russell became the first player to dunk regularly, although without any of the current fancy moves.

Russell's shortened rookie season of on-the-job learning in 1956–57 became an education to other teams. He averaged nearly 15 points and

Celtics center Bill Russell leaps high into the air on his way to one of his famous slam dunks.

20 rebounds per game. The Philadelphia Warriors' owner, Eddie Gottlieb, asked the league to stop the young shot blocker from committing "legal goal-tending" while playing a "one-man zone"!

Teams Wilt Over Wilt

Russell's unique style of play sent his opponents scrambling for new game plans. That's why, in 1959, Philadelphia owner Gottlieb chose 7-foot-1 Wilt Chamberlain as his top draft pick. Gottlieb hoped his newcomer could work the same defensive magic Russell created. (The Warriors won rights to Chamberlain because he was born in Philadelphia and attended high school there. In the 1950s, the NBA offered teams "territorial" picks so they could increase ticket sales by using native players, or players who had played college ball in that city.)

The wishes of the Warriors' owner came true. On November 24, 1960, Chamberlain battled Boston's Russell on the backboards, collecting a record 55 rebounds. Philadelphia never knew such a workhorse. In 1961, Chamberlain played in a record 79 complete games, never sitting out a minute. On March 2, 1962, "Wilt the Stilt" scored 100 points against the New York Knicks, which would add to his record collection of 4,029 points for the season. Amazingly, he never fouled out in 1,045 career games. And Chamberlain did become Bill Russell's greatest rival during the 1960s.

Chamberlain helped the Philadelphia 76ers to victory against Russell's Celtics in the 1967 NBA Eastern Division Finals, ending Boston's eight-year run as champions. Russell was serving his first year as player-coach, becoming the first black head coach in any American professional league. But Chamberlain's lack of scoring provides a clue to Philadelphia's title. A year earlier, Wilt led the NBA with 33.5 points per game average. While he dropped to 24.1 points per game, Cham-

> **George Mikan** didn't make his high-school team, partly because the coach said, "You can't play with glasses on." However, Mikan kept playing. After college, he played for the Lakers. The Lakers won five titles in six years. Mikan led the NBA in scoring three times—glasses and all.

berlain averaged a league-best 24 rebounds per game and 7.8 assists, third in the NBA. More defense made the difference.

Not long after Chamberlain's star faded, another big man lit up basketball's center sky. Lew Alcindor, 7 foot 2, joined the Milwaukee Bucks for 1969–70. One year later, Alcindor adopted the Muslim name the hoops world will remember forever: Kareem Abdul-Jabbar. His NBA career would include six championship rings and six Most Valuable

Wilt Chamberlain of the Philadelphia Warriors and Bill Russell of the Boston Celtics started their intense rivalry in 1960.

> Gheorghe Muresan, basketball's 7-foot-7 Romanian, isn't bashful about his size. He abbreviates it on his jersey: number 77.

Player awards. Jabbar's old-fashioned hook shot was renamed a "sky hook" by a media overwhelmed by his size and grace. Upon his retirement, Abdul-Jabbar had blocked 3,189 shots in 1,560 games, leading the league three times. He remained for years the NBA's all-time career scoring leader with 38,387 points, which included only one three-point field goal.

Abdul-Jabbar reinforced what centers would need to do as the 20th century ended. Size matters. Becoming planted in the lane stops fast breaks. Living near the basket helps in "posting up" for close turnaround shots, while providing great position for rebounds. Because the other team's center will camp near the hoop, that's where the one-on-one battle begins. Most of all, Abdul-Jabbar's 5,000-plus assists showed that a center could feed outside shooters.

Another player near the end of his career was the first to show the many ways a center could serve a team, all in one game. In 1974, Nate Thurmond owned more than a decade of NBA experience. Yet, despite the common belief that youth equals strength, Thurmond became the first to post a "quadruple double." His 22 points, 14 rebounds, 13 assists, and 12 blocked shots meant that Thurmond topped double figures in four major categories, both offensive and defensive.

Is Size Enough?

In the 1980s NBA teams kept testing the game plan that "bigger is better." The 1985 Washington Bullets discovered 7-foot-7 Manute Bol from Sudan. The league went to new heights in introducing Bol, the biggest center ever: Sportswriters described to fans how the African had killed a lion with his bare hands as a teen!

Unfortunately, neither Bol's size nor his past was a huge factor in his NBA success. Joining the NBA after a freshman season at a small Connecticut college, Bol set a record by blocking 397 shots as a rookie. Two times in his first two years he blocked 15 shots in a game. But after nine seasons with four teams, he never surpassed an average of four points per game. Like basketball's earliest teams, Bol's teams had to learn that centers should do more than block shots.

Yet teams continue to seek size in their centers. Houston rocketed to the NBA Finals in 1986, building on a game plan of "twin towers." That's what the media dubbed the starting lineup of 7-foot-4 Ralph Sampson and 7-foot rookie Hakeem Olajuwon. They soared to the Finals, only to be toppled by Boston in six games.

Unlike Washington's Bol, Olajuwon and the current crop of imported centers have dazzled observers with their footwork. Many of these foreign-born big men developed their surprising mobility in another sport: soccer. And once grace gets them into good defensive positions, these centers use their size as a roadblock for opponents.

Don't think that only basketball's skyscrapers can make decent centers. At 6 foot 9, Dave Cowens might seem like a flea by current center standards. Still, he made Boston a capable center for 10 years, the last as a player-coach. The Celtics secured two championships (1974 and 1976) with Cowens in the middle. He gained Hall of Fame membership in 1990.

Even Cowens towered over 6-foot-7 center Wes Unseld, a 13-year veteran with the Bullets (now Wizards). Unseld was famed for his passing, a talent not many other 1970s centers shared. Unseld joined the Hall of Fame in 1987.

Sure, several extra inches might make work as an NBA center easier. Still, courage, muscle, and a solid background in basketball fundamentals are the best yardsticks to measure centers of any size with.

> "I don't dunk unless I have to. I guess you've got to have some kind of flair, and I don't."
> — Nate Thurmond
>
> Thurmond was too humble. In 1984 he was elected to the Basketball Hall of Fame.

4 GOING FORWARD

Forward march!

A team with two talented forwards has a good chance of marching to post-season play. Today's starting lineups usually feature a "small forward" and a "power forward."

A small forward often isn't as tall as the power forward. However, a small forward has big responsibilities. A shooter who can hit from around the court makes a good small forward. Detroit's Grant Hill is an example.

For more than a decade, the NBA viewed one man as the textbook example of a small forward. Boston's Larry Bird played from 1979 to 1992. In 13 seasons, he made 12 all-star teams and was inducted into the Hall of Fame in 1998. Bird didn't seem to be the fastest player, nor was he the greatest leaper. Yet he averaged 24 points per game and revived the Celtics passing game, while exceeding 100 steals per season for a decade.

Small forward Julius Erving didn't dazzle the NBA immediately. He began a five-year run with the American Basketball Association in 1971. When the ABA became part of the NBA, Erving fueled the Philadelphia 76ers from 1976 to 1987. "Dr. J's" game plan called for more than uncorking slam dunks. His 1981 NBA Most Valuable Player award proves that he was an all-around player. Erving's leadership on both offense and defense paved the way for Philadelphia's 1983 championship.

When elected to the Hall of Fame in 1992, Erving's 30,026 points were the most ever for a non-center. Only Wilt Chamberlain and Kareem Abdul-Jabbar had scored more.

The first small forward known as an offensive machine was Laker Elgin Baylor, who played from 1958 to 1972. Baylor flew to the hoop, launching airborne moves unseen in his era. John Castellani, a former Lakers' coach, said, "Elgin has more moves than a clock." In 1960, before Chamberlain's 100-point game record, Baylor held history briefly with 71 points in one outing versus the Knicks. A year earlier, he busted Boston with a historic 64-point show. For his career, Baylor averaged 27 points per game.

Scottie Pippen's traditional position with Chicago's 1990s championship teams was small forward. Pippen took center stage following teammate Michael Jordan's 1993 temporary retirement. The world learned Pippen's full potential in the 1994 NBA All-Star game. He poured in 29 points in 31 minutes, including five three-pointers, winning the game's MVP award. Despite being only 6 foot 7, Pippen seems to play all positions, guarding any opposing player.

Most frontcourts are rounded out by a power forward, who may seem like a second center. In fact, some power forwards

Julius Erving was known as "Dr. J" because of his intelligent leadership on both offense and defense. Wearing number 6, he played for the Philadelphia 76ers from 1976 to 1987.

are former centers whose nimble ballhandling skills made them better suited for the new position. Utah's Karl Malone shows how the position is played, muscling to the basket for close shots and plenty of rebounds. During his college career, Malone became known as the "Mailman," because he delivered on the court!

Barkley's Behind

Two power forwards gained fame for their rebounding in the 1990s. Charles Barkley, perhaps small for the position at 6 foot 6, used his seat as a weapon in playing the boards. Even though age lessened Barkley's leaping skill, taller players couldn't reach over and around Barkley when he used his behind as a screen to keep foes at bay.

Dennis "Worm" Rodman won his creepy nickname for the way he'd slither between players for the ball. A league-leading rebounder for most of the decade, Rodman's secret was in his fingertips. He couldn't always grab control of a loose ball, but would tip it away from anyone else, into open territory.

The tradition of power forward is far from new. Bob Pettit refined the role with the St. Louis (now Atlanta) Hawks, playing from 1954 to 1965. The 11-time all-star and two-time MVP topped 20,000 points, and posted a career rebound average of more than 16 per game. Yet as a high school sophomore, Pettit was cut from the team!

> When a player starts a fast break with a one-handed, overhand throw, the basketball term is a "baseball pass." However, the ball is thrown more like a quarterback throwing a football.

Looking back on his career, Pettit explained that he expected to score 8 to 12 points per game from offensive rebounds. Near the basket, he first checked where his rebounding foe was. Pettit would block out the opponent before watching the ball hit the rim.

"I held my arms up and my elbows out when I jumped. Usually, my elbows were over my defender's shoulders, so when he jumped for a rebound, he carried me up with him," Pettit said.

Like Bob Pettit, other forwards have been overlooked in hoops history. Alex English retired in 1991 with little fanfare, despite more than 25,000 points in his career.

Small forward Dominique Wilkins spent 11 fruitless years with Atlanta (1983–94), waiting for the championship that never came. The 6-foot-8 scorer did his part, earning eight all-star selections. He surpassed English's milestone, becoming history's highest-scoring

Bob Pettit (center) is an outstanding example of a power forward. Playing with the St. Louis Hawks from 1954 to 1965, he was one of the top scorers in professional basketball.

forward with more than 24,000 points. Others higher on the lifetime points ladder spent part of their careers at center or guard.

Wilkins was dubbed the "Human Highlights Film" for his mind-boggling dunks. Still, the man born in Paris, France, showed that a forward could be a complete player. Versus the world champion Bulls in 1992, Wilkins sank a record 23 free throws in one game, without a single miss.

Forward Thinking

Forward Rick Barry powered the underrated Golden State Warriors to a 1975 NBA championship. Combine his four-year scoring total in the rival American Basketball Association with his 10 years in the NBA, and the 6-foot-7 Barry surpasses 25,000 career points.

"The most fun about playing the game is when every possession is a critical possession," Barry said. "That's where all the time and confidence pays off; it's what separates the good players from the great players. The good players won't do as well in those tight situations where every play is crucial." Besides, Barry pointed out, "It's not as much fun when you're beating someone by 28 or 30 points."

Barry loved a close game, but admitted, "I was not an easy person to play with because I was a perfectionist. I expected the best from myself at every game, and I expected nothing less from the people on my team. But the guys who knew me knew that that was only on the court."

But no matter how intimidating Barry sometimes seemed to his teammates, "If a guy is open, he gets the ball whether I like him or not," Barry said. "A great player is a team player, one who puts the goals of the team ahead of the goal of the individual. You can't be selfish. It's a team sport.

> **A "three-point play" is not a three-point shot. For a three-point play, a player must be fouled in the act of shooting. If the basket goes in, the player still gets one free throw. If it's good, the total is three. The moral: Follow through on every shot, even if you hear the referee's whistle.**

"If anyone wants to be great in this game, they have to give their best every time, every game, every play. If you're not willing to give your best, you'll never be great."

Barry continued giving to the game even after he retired: His sons—Jon, Drew, and Brent Barry—all played NBA ball in the 1990s. But even with a famous father, it seems only some players are born forwards. Jon, Drew, and Brent are all guards!

5 ON GUARD

New fans may get the wrong idea that a "point guard" has something to do with scoring points. But point guards get their name from serving as the "point" of the offense, where every game plan begins.

Point guards are also described as playmakers, the quarterbacks of a basketball team. When coaches diagram plays with numbers to represent players, they call their point guards "one guards." That's because most plays start with the point guard, who brings the ball up court. (Shooting guards are "twos," small forwards are "threes," power forwards are "fours," and centers are "fives.")

On many plays, fans won't see a point guard near the basket. Smart point guards will hover near the top of the key (the half-circle behind the free-throw lane). From there, the point can reset the play after an offensive rebound. Good floor position means the point is ready to

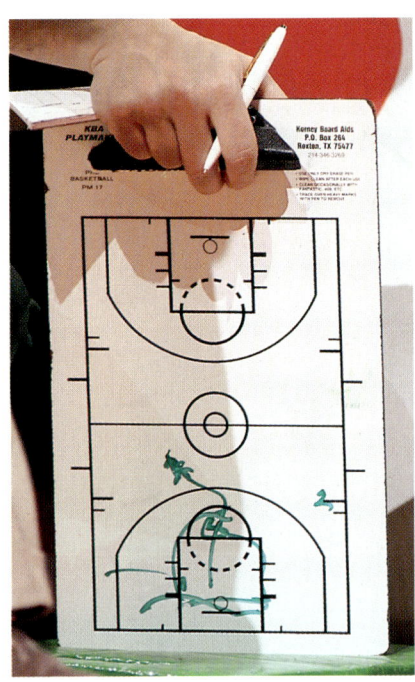

A play board showing a diagrammed play for a 1996 game between the Boston Celtics and the Philadelphia 76ers

play defense after a basket. The work never lets up for a second: A point guard caught off-guard could give up an easy fast break off a floor-length pass. That's why SuperSonic Gary Payton sticks so close to the opponent with the ball; fans and teammates call him "Glove"—he fits himself to opponents snug as a glove.

Directing the offense means a talented point guard will be handing out assists like Halloween candy. Handling the ball is one of the point's main jobs. Boston—and the NBA—learned the power of the point guard from Bob Cousy, a fixture from 1950 to 1963. After 6,955 assists and 16,960 points, the basketball world proclaimed Cousy "Houdini of the Hardwood," after the famous escape artist.

> "Elbows knocked out far more teeth than punches."
>
> — Don Barksdale, NBA player, 1951–55, on how dangerous getting a rebound could be.

Going into the 1997 Finals, only three championship teams had ever possessed point guards who led their teams in scoring. Earvin "Magic" Johnson was the first, topping the 1987 Lakers with a 23.9 average. Johnson's reflexes and smarts on the floor made him a famed point guard, even though he didn't look the part. The 6-foot-9 Laker towered above many point guards in the league. (Often, a team's point guard is its shortest player.)

The Lakers needed "Magic" in the sixth game of the 1980 NBA Finals against Philadelphia. The tall point guard, then a rookie, substituted for injured center Kareem Abdul-Jabbar. Johnson rang up 42 points in the strange position, securing a title for Los Angeles.

"Magic" didn't own the all-time assists record for long. While other teams were winning championships, Utah point guard John Stockton rewrote two chapters of basketball history. Not only did the Jazz workhorse become the NBA's all-time assists leader, he grabbed the career steals mark, too.

Like Johnson, Stockton is a professor of assists. Both players could amaze opponents with no-look or behind-the-back passes to set up scores. However, both men were also artists with the basic two-handed pass from the chest. They knew that, just like an often-intercepted quarterback, a player who cocks his arm for a one-handed pass can reveal his aims.

Driven to Dribble

From Cousy to Johnson, point guards know the importance of ballhandling in any game plan. Point guard Scott Skiles played some of his first ball as a kid on a dirt court. His father always checked to see how dirty Scott's palms were at the end of playing. Why? The best dribbling is done with fingertips, providing for the best control.

Brent Price of the Houston Rockets in a power drive dribbles past an opposing player.

Steve Alford played on the 1984 gold medal U.S. Olympic team and later for four years in the NBA. The point guard polished his dribbling skills everywhere. "I used to dribble a ball around our yard at home. The neighbors thought I was crazy, but it really helped me," he said. "I dribbled through a rock bed one summer to improve my fingertip control."

Where there's a one, a two can't be far behind. In basketball, the "two guard" has the unofficial name of "shooting guard." For shooting guards, one of the first to shine at the position was Jerry West of the Lakers. He was known as "Mr. Clutch," averaging more than 29 points a game in 153 play-off appearances. In 14 seasons in Los Angeles, he scored more than 25,000 points.

Fans of the 1990s knew West as the Lakers' general manager, responsible for moves like signing free-agent center Shaquille O'Neal. Yet West the player made even greater moves. "He had hands that were as quick as a snake's tongue," said Lenny Wilkens, the NBA's winningest coach, who retired as a point guard in 1975 with a then-record 7,211 assists. Wilkens described West's defense, saying, "I wished they had kept tracks of steals when Jerry and I played, because we would have been the league leaders."

> **Knicks guard John Starks might have been the star who never was. No one drafted Starks in 1988 after college. The Warriors let him go after 36 games. He played a year in the Continental Basketball Association before finding his home in New York and becoming an all-star.**

The Greatest Guard?

Then came Chicago's Michael Jordan, a shooting guard named the greatest player ever by sportswriters voting for the NBA's 50th anniversary celebration in 1997. (Shockingly, as a 5-foot-9 sophomore, Jordan was cut from his high-school team!) With the Bulls, Jordan proved that his position has the right name. The shooting guard is supposed to shoot. The biggest three-point makers in the NBA often are shooting guards. Not surprisingly, the best shooters do it with either hand.

Jack Twyman, a six-time NBA all-star elected to the Hall of Fame in 1982, spent more time as forward than guard. No matter where he played, he played to shoot. "The single most important aspect of my confidence in taking the shot under any circumstances came as a result of long hours of practice," he said. "On my own, I would shoot a minimum of 500 practice shots a day."

Shooting and scoring depends on who has the ball. Following Jordan's lead, current stars at shooting guard have polished smooth moves for whenever they *don't* have the ball.

Michael Jordan (center) is a shooting guard expert in rebounding as well as making baskets. Here he grabs a rebound from in front of Atlanta Hawks Steve Smith in a May 1997 game in Chicago.

"Cuts" are the key for such court travel. This basketball term for escaping a defender only hints at how a shooting guard can remove himself to become the open man. To see this skill in full form, watch how a guard like Jordan can get off a shot, then rebound his own miss for a second shot attempt. With or without the ball, guards slip through court traffic, undetected.

Guard Steve Smith entered the NBA as a first-round draft pick of the Miami Heat in 1991. "Everyone's talent is about the same in the pros," he said. "What keeps you here is the time you put in studying and practicing longer."

As the point or the shooter, Smith has the right game plan to stay on guard.

> **"Cheryl! Cheryl!"**
>
> — *The call of fans in Chicago during the 1997–98 play-offs to distract guard Reggie Miller of the Indiana Pacers while he shot free throws. Miller's older sister, Cheryl Miller, is a WNBA coach and Hall of Famer.*

6 OFF THE BENCH

The nonstarter, the "sixth man," the substitute—these are a few of the names given to the players asked to come off the bench to maintain a lead or rally a comeback. A sixth man has to be ready to do every job on the team, at any second.

Maybe the reserve needs to let a player in foul trouble cool off. Instead of having a center or an important defender like Dennis Rodman lost early in the game from fouling out, a key substitute will be asked to keep his team in the game for a few minutes. That way, the starter can return to win the game in the decisive final minutes.

Oddly, the NBA didn't honor these star substitutes until after the 1982–83 season, when the Sixth Man award was created. Writers and broadcasters now vote for a winner. The first super-sub honored was Philadelphia's Bobby Jones.

With the 76ers in 1981–82, the 6-foot-9 Jones started in 73 of his 76 games played. It was the first time in eight pro seasons that Jones was a starter. His numbers were decent, averaging more than 14 points and five rebounds per game. But the following year, Philadelphia signed free-agent Moses Malone. Malone would become the league MVP. With Julius "Dr. J" Erving as the resident star, the 76ers needed room for Malone in their lineup. They made room by saving Jones as the sub for Philly's two big men. Jones was a big help, averaging 23 minutes and nine points per game. Sitting for the good of the team helped the 76ers, who won that year's championship against the Lakers.

Fans often think of a sixth man as a younger player ready to become a starter, someone needing experience. That wasn't the case for Bobby Jones, or Bill Walton, who won the Sixth Man award for Boston in 1985–86. The L.A. Clippers had traded the injury-plagued 33-year-old, thinking his best days were gone. But the 7-foot Walton played in 80 games for Boston, providing breathers for starters Robert Parish and Kevin McHale. McHale, by the way, had been the NBA's sixth man for the two seasons prior, working his way into Boston's starting lineup. With McHale and Walton, the Celtics sailed to an NBA crown.

The Bench Begins

Historians say that another Celtic created the sixth man concept. Frank Ramsey played off the bench for Boston for nine seasons, from 1954 to 1964. He averaged only 24 minutes per game, but averaged 13.4 points per game, earning Hall of Fame honors in 1981.

"The ultimate sixth man is a guy who can make an immediate impact in the game, both offensively and defensively, and do it at guard or forward. That was Frank's role, and then he taught it to me," said John Havlicek.

When Havlicek was Boston's top draft pick in 1962, Coach Auerbach wanted a replacement for Ramsey, who would soon be retiring with aching knees. Havlicek

Part of a good game plan is having a reliable substitute—a sixth man—ready to come off the bench to relieve a starting player or to give a fresh charge to a game. Bobby Jones did an excellent job for the 76ers as a sixth man.

Frank Ramsey refined the role of the sixth man for the Boston Celtics, playing off the bench for nine seasons.

> Coaches love a player who is in "triple threat" position. That player is controlling the ball with proper footwork and body position, ready to dribble, pass, or shoot.

learned to play different positions, and to follow Auerbach's directive for the sixth man: Score quickly!

History may someday say that Portland's bench helped shape the Chicago Bulls' dynasty. How? The Trailblazers couldn't fit rookie Clyde "The Glide" Drexler into their starting lineup in 1983–84, due to guard Jim Paxson's presence. When Michael Jordan became available in the following season's college draft, Portland saw Drexler on their bench and decided against signing yet another young guard who might struggle to get playing time. They selected 7-foot-1 center Sam Bowie. Choosing next, the Bulls picked the leftover Jordan.

Drexler advanced to the starting lineup the next year, gaining his share of fame. Yet Trailblazers fans can't help imagining superstar Jordan in a Portland uniform (even as a sixth man!).

Subs Save Bulls

Great teams have great benches. That fact was proven in 1992. In Game five of the NBA Finals, Chicago trailed Portland, 79–64. After three quarters, coach Phil Jackson had enough. He pulled Michael Jordan and three other starters, leaving Scottie Pippen with substitutes Bobby Hansen, Stacey King, B.J. Armstrong, and Scott Williams. The Trailblazers were outscored, 14–2. With the

> "He must have three lungs!"
>
> — *New York opponent Dick Barnett, joking about how Boston's John Havlicek never seemed to tire during a game.*

lead reduced to 81–78, Jackson returned to his standard lineup. The Bulls won, 119–106, and would win the title in a sixth game.

"It's either daring or stupid, depending on which way it comes out," Jackson told reporters later. "We needed a different match-up." Although none of the four subs wound up as leading scorers, they allowed Jordan and the first team time to rest and regroup.

Jackson's success stems from mining his bench for all its riches. When the 1995–96 Bulls made history with a 72–10 mark on the way to a fourth championship, Chicago's Toni Kukoc won the Sixth Man award. Both coach and player gave unusual responses to the news.

"It's a nice award, a great award," Kukoc told reporters. "But I still want to be in the starting lineup. I still want to play. That's not a secret." Jackson told *USA TODAY*, "Toni has accepted the role, but he's not happy with it. I'm pleased he's not, to be honest. The fact that Toni thinks he's a star, believes he's a star, is important."

Of course, not all the best nonstarters believe that substituting is second-best.

Bob McAdoo had played nearly 10 years in the NBA, winning three scoring titles and an MVP award. But he had played for five different teams. Some rumors claimed McAdoo was a selfish player who'd rather score than help his team win. Who wanted a player like that?

The Lakers hired him in December 1981. In four seasons with Los Angeles, he played in four NBA Finals, helping win two championships. "With the Lakers, I knew I didn't have to carry the entire load," McAdoo said. "They already had a great

> There's no showstopping assist like the "alley-oop." A player leaps to the hoop, ready to dunk. But where's the ball? It's coming! A teammate's pass puts the ball near the hoop, and the airborne player does the rest.

• 41 •

scorer in Kareem. And Magic Johnson was doing his thing. I could relax and just play my game. There wasn't a lot of pressure to score."

Whether a sixth man accepts the job for a lifetime or just one game, substitutes and starters become equals on the court. Both are looking for a moment of glory. And off the court, they both wait for that moment in the next game.

BASKETBALL BASICS

When a coach talks about a player's "mechanics," he isn't discussing who fixes cars. The coach is talking about how a player performs the different movements needed in each part of a play.

A game plan is built with plays, and plays are built on mechanics, or fundamentals. One of the most exciting plays is the three-point shot, when a player launches a long-distance ball.

In Jack Twyman's 11-year career, he scored 15,840 points (a 19.2 average)—all before the three-point rule. "I shot a lot of outside shots, so I expect that if the 3-point shot was in effect, my total point output would have been significantly greater," he said.

Since the 1979–80 season, the NBA has offered players the choice of scoring more than the standard two-pointer, if they shoot from outside a 23-foot, 9-inch arc. Once known as "gunning," shooting at impossible-looking targets, today's three-point shooters are more scientific.

Referees must watch the shooting player's feet. If the shooter begins with both feet outside the circle, three points will result. The ref will signal by raising an arm in the air, complete with three outstretched fingers. Players call the three-pointer a "trey," from the French word for three. In today's NBA, nearly one-third of shots taken come from behind the three-point arc. Players who convert even half of their three-point shots are seen as magicians.

> Look through the rim. That circle is 18 inches in diameter. Measure the width of a basketball. That's only 9 inches in diameter. Smaller ball, bigger hoop, but they don't always fit together!

The three-point shot is an uncomplicated surprise, unlike the slam dunk. Call it a jam or stuff, it can be one-handed, two-handed, or a reverse. What doesn't change is the power shown by a player who leaps through a tangle of bodies and above the 10-foot-high basket to drive the ball through the hoop.

Big men like Shaquille O'Neal seem to carry rival players on their backs as they soar above the rim. Often, opponents will be caught standing in a player's path, where they hope to halt the oncoming dunker and draw a charging foul. Or a defender might foul the player in mid-slam. Unlike an airborne ball, the dunk is a tough-to-block play because the scorer-to-be never lets go of the ball. In either case, the hope is to make the player earn his two points the harder way, with a pair of free throws.

Players above 7 feet make dunks look easy, as if they need to take only a tiny hop to float above the rim. Yet any player with leaping ability has the chance at a dunk, regardless of how tall he is. Five-foot-three "Muggsy" Bogues and 5-foot-7 "Spud" Webb seemed to fly through a forest of taller players to slam.

From 1984 through 1996, the NBA All-Star game featured a pregame contest of slam dunks, a "dunk-a-thon" of sorts. Players would unveil fancy moves, anything from dunking two balls in one leap to dunking blindfolded. Another pregame exhibition that survives is a three-point shoot-off. Craig Hodges, then with the Bulls, slipped from the shadow of Michael Jordan's fame, winning the three-point contest in three different years.

One Point at a Time

When it comes to field goals, players have to fight for a chance for their three-point or two-point shots. That's why free throws have remained at one point throughout basketball history. After all, players get to shoot from only 15 feet away, whenever they're ready, with no one standing in their path. The term "charity stripe" is sometimes used to describe the free-throw line. Then why does free-throw shooting seem so hard for some players?

For the 1997–98 season, Michael Jordan and Shaquille O'Neal were neck and neck as NBA scoring leaders. What made the difference? Jordan sank more free throws. "It's just all concentration," O'Neal told reporters, explaining his problems at the line.

O'Neal wasn't alone in his free-throw frustration. More than one third of the NBA made 8 of every 10 free throws in 1973. Twenty-five years later, the group of 80 percent-successful shooters shrank by some 8 percent.

There is no one way to become a top free-throw shooter. Rick Barry, who was elected to the Hall of Fame in 1986, sank 90 percent of his free throws in a 15-year career—all underhand!

"My father played and coached semi-pro teams, and he got me to try it [the underhand method of free-throw] when I was in high school. When you're making 80 percent of your free throws, coaches don't bother you about how you're doing it," Barry said. "Sure, some kids teased me about how I looked, but they knew, too, that you look kind of stupid making fun of someone when [he's] making the baskets."

Houston's Calvin Murphy once sank 78 free throws in a row. He sank a record

L.A. Lakers Shaquille O'Neal displays great leaping ability as he goes up for a slam dunk.

> Gym teacher James Naismith taught the game he invented to some of his students in 1891. The baskets were peach baskets, nailed to the gym balcony. Naismith created 13 rules, but his rules never spoke of dribbling.

95.8 percent of his free-throw tries in 1980–81. Murphy, only 5 foot 9, credited his free-throw talent to skills he learned from his off-court hobby: baton twirling!

"Pistol" Pete Maravich gained his nickname from taking more shots than a gun. Playing from 1970 to 1980, he sank a decent 82 percent of his free throws. Some fans thought his long, floppy socks were pointless—until he went to the line. Maravich dried his sweaty hands on his drooping socks before all free-throw attempts.

True fans know there's more to the game than scoring. Oddly, the NBA failed to mention much else for its first 20 years.

The league wanted stars, and stressed offense. So, in the beginning, reporters told mostly about a player's minutes played and points averaged. Not until the 1973–74 season did the NBA expand the types of statistics it kept. Rebounds would be divided into offensive and defensive rebounds. Steals would be compiled. Blocked shots would be noted, too.

Suddenly, fans began to watch more than the score. Once-ignored numbers seemed more important after new stats were added. One category that regained interest was the assist. In other words, which player assisted the scorer? Just like a football quarterback, the player who gains an assist has found an "open man," a possible shooter who's escaped a defender and is ready to score.

Utah point guard John Stockton sneaked up on hoops history in the 1990s. The all-time assists leader became the first in basketball to pass out more than 12,000 scoring opportunities.

No Law Against Steals

But the act that steals the show every time has got to be the steal, the act of taking the ball away from the offense. In the 1965 NBA Eastern Division Finals, fans realized how important this play can be.

"Havlicek stole the ball! It's all over! It's all over!" screamed Boston announcer Johnny Most. John Havlicek's Celtics beat Philadelphia, 110-109. "Hondo" deflected an inbounds pass, and teammate Sam Jones cashed in on a quick layup as time ran out. In his career, Havlicek collected at least 476 steals. But just looking at "new" stats finally kept during the last five years of the aging veteran's career, Havlicek's skill is proven with an average of more than one interception per game.

The league has kept searching for ways to measure a player's and a team's success. Even stats that do not make players look good are included. Individual turnovers were recorded beginning in 1977. Did the player throw the ball away? Did someone else steal the ball? If so, it's TO—turnover—time.

Don't be surprised if new stats appear in basketball's future. Love them or hate them, the basics of basketball will keep being studied with numbers. Put all those statistical building blocks together, and coaches have the stuff to build a winning game plan.

John Havlicek, who played for the Boston Celtics in the 1960s, was a master of stealing the ball and intercepting passes.

8 DEVASTATING DUOS

Seven seasons after the 1991 NBA Finals were called "The Magic and Michael Show," Michael Jordan's Bulls were in the Finals again, this time versus the Utah Jazz. During those years, Jordan had added four championship rings to his first, and "Michael and his supporting cast" had become "Michael and Scottie and their supporting cast," according to *USA TODAY*.

In 1998 Jordan and Scottie Pippen were the only two Bulls to play on all five Bulls championship teams. "The harmony between the two of us is incomparable," Jordan told *USA TODAY*, which agreed that "Jordan's unstoppable offense [and] Pippen's irrepressible defense" made the pair "devastating."

But the Utah Jazz had a devastating duo of its own. Karl Malone and John Stockton had been together since 1985 and were famous for perfecting the "pick-and-roll." When power guard Stockton had the ball, Malone would set a "pick" for him, blocking the path of Stockton's defender so Stockton could pass the ball, then move into scoring position. When Malone finally "rolled" off the pick, freeing the defense so it could try to stop Stockton, the ball was quickly thrown to the open Malone for the score.

Sometimes Stockton helped set the pick for 6-foot-9, 255-pound Malone, who scored by muscling his way to the basket. Sometimes Malone and teammates set picks for the smaller Stockton, who shot elegantly

Utah Jazz John Stockton goes up for a basket between Chicago Bulls Michael Jordan (left) and Scottie Pippen in Game 5 of the 1998 NBA Finals.

from three-point range. The Jazz would often feed the ball to Malone a few times in a row, so opponents would forget to look for Stockton's shot.

The Bulls' offensive master plan was famous, too. Assistant coach Tex Winter's "Triangle" spaced the Bulls around the court, making it difficult for the Jazz to double-team anyone: After all, if two Jazz were on Jordan, Scottie Pippen or Toni Kukoc might be left wide open, and that was not a good idea. Even if those stars missed their shots, the Bulls went after rebounds like bulldogs. Chicago's defense was dogged, too: As the series got under way, Pippen took charge after charge from Malone as Utah tried to drive to the basket.

> An NBA game is played in one time zone. However, the half-court line is known as the "time line." Cross half-court 10 seconds after gaining possession, or lose the ball.

Rewriting History

History seemed to be on the side of the Bulls, who had won five championships in seven years with their techniques—1991, 1992, 1993, 1996, and 1997. But, strangely, history was on Utah's side, too: Utah was the team that had taken the Bulls to the Finals in 1997 and lost. The last five times a next-year rematch had occurred, the losing team had always taken revenge.

Utah won the first game, and Chicago took the second. But "it's almost like one long game," Bulls' center Luc Longley said. "The longer the game goes on, the more you see of it and the more you understand it."

Both of those first games had been close. But Longley's words seemed to come true in the third game, the most lopsided in NBA Finals history. With the Bulls at home for the first time that series, Chicago blew Utah out of the water, 96–54. They did it with defense. "Defense," Bulls players liked to say, "wins championships."

They'd stifled the pick-and-roll by keeping Stockton and Malone well guarded, sticking with those two, never leaving them alone. Jazz passes were intercepted, drives were blocked. Utah, said Chicago's Steve Kerr, relied on "a point-guard dominated offense." He meant, of course, John Stockton. "They really want the ball in that point guard's hands."

"We're starting to run them out of their sets," Scottie Pippen agreed.

Utah seemed to need drastic measures. But Jazz star Jeff Hornacek said, "You can't change your offense all of a sudden. We looked at the tape and saw that the things they were doing weren't that big a deal."

The primary change the Jazz made in Game 4 was putting Adam Keefe in the starting line-up to shadow Pippen, who had been the Bulls' "floating" defense, using his own on-court judgment to double-team where he saw the most need. When Utah's Keefe kept Pippen under control, Stockton's scoring buoyed, and the game was a good, tight one. But even though Chicago was the team called for illegal defense, it was Utah that got into foul trouble, sending Chicago to the free-throw line for 40 shots. The Bulls made 27 of those.

> He was a walk-on for his Iowa State team, playing without a scholarship. He was the 46th chosen in the NBA draft in 1986. But Jeff Hornacek kept shooting. In the 1997 All-Star game, he was basketball's three-point champion as a popular member of the Utah Jazz.

"All the teams that win championships, especially Chicago, hit their free throws down the stretch," New York Knicks' center Herb Williams told *Sports Illustrated*. "During the course of the game, you might not notice it, but at the end of the game it shows up." It did in Game 4: Chicago won again, by a much closer 86–82.

The Jazz was behind in the series, with one win to Chicago's three. No team had ever come back from such a deficit to clinch a series, and Utah still had one more night away from home in the Windy City—a city that was ready to celebrate as soon as Game 5 was done.

Drastic Measures

Utah had just one chance to stay alive. To do it, they did change their offense. Utah's pick-and-roll was seen less in Game 5 and the inside game was seen more—much more. Malone stayed near the basket, taking his team's feeds and daring Chicago to rack up defensive fouls as his scoring soared to 39 points. Trying to stop him, Pippen did foul out, with only six points. Yet Pippen said the Jazz player who "made the difference in the game" was substitute Antoine Carr. Carr's 12 points for the night included some sweet free throws in a close fourth quarter.

> Teammates help each other, on and off the court. Cincinnati Royal Maurice Stokes became ill and paralyzed in 1958. Teammate Jack Twyman became his legal guardian, helping to pay all his medical bills.

Like Pippen, Jordan's game was off, too. His botched three-pointer at the buzzer left Chicago empty-handed for a championship celebration as Utah stayed afloat for the win, 83–81. The final Finals would take place back in Salt Lake City, Utah.

It looked as if those last games might be without Pippen. The night of Game 6, Pippen's back pain was plain in every step he took. He agreed to let team doctors give him a strong shot before the game so he could play. But after Pippen's first dunk, "the pain just started building from that point on," he said later. Pippen played anyway, scoring 8 points, three rebounds, four assists, two steals, and a blocked shot. "I knew I just wanted to come back [and] help our team stay in the game." He believed that if he could even come out onto the floor, "my presence would be all-important." Pippen was right—the Bulls needed every shred of support in this tense matchup. Even with Jordan's 45 points, the

In Game 5 of the 1998 NBA Finals, Utah Jazz forward Karl Malone (left) was game high scorer with 39 points, beating Michael Jordan's score by 1 point.

game was anybody's right up to MJ's last-minute game-winning basket in the 87–86 victory. But to many, Pippen's performance was the highlight of the Finals.

A game plan gives players a way to win, but no one can give them a will to win. A good strategy doesn't always win games. Neither does a strong will. But put the two together, and championships can be won. The Bulls saw that even after five championship rings, Pippen still wanted to win. If he could play hard, they could play hard.

"I think, that of all the championships we've won, this is the toughest," Michael Jordan said.

The toughest games are the sweetest won.

In an intense, highly competitive game with a championship on the line, sometimes it can get a little rough. A good game plan helps, but ultimately it is the players who provide the win or loss.

GLOSSARY

alley-oop: when one player throws the ball toward the basket and a teammate by the hoop leaps up to help the ball in.
assist: passing to a teammate, who then makes a basket.
backcourt: the side of the court where a team is playing defense. Players who are guards are also called "the backcourt." (See **frontcourt**.)
bank shot: when a ball bounces off the backboard and into the basket.
baseline: the out-of-bounds line behind the basket. Also called endline.
block: when a defensive player makes illegal bodily contact with an opponent. Also, when a player stops an opponent's shot in midair.
block out: when a defensive player uses his or her body to keep an opponent away from a rebound. Also called box out or screen.
blocked shot: when a defensive player stops a ball that an opponent has shot toward the basket.
board: rebound.
bounce pass: passing to a teammate by bouncing the ball on the floor.
breakaway: when a player steals the ball, then speeds to his or her own basket before the other team can catch up.
brick: a clumsy, unsuccessful shot.
carrying: a violation resulting from a player not keeping the palm of the hand toward the floor while dribbling the ball.
center: a center scores close to the basket when playing offense. On defense, the center usually grabs rebounds and blocks shots.
charge: when a defensive player is holding still in a set position, and an offensive player runs into him or her.

defense: the team without the ball, which is trying to get the ball and keep the team with the ball from scoring.

double dribble: to use both hands at the same time while dribbling (bounce the ball while running). To stop dribbling, then start again, is also a double dribble.

double-team: when two defensive players guard the same opponent.

dribble: to bounce the ball. Players are allowed to take two steps per bounce.

fast break: when a defensive player grabs an opponent's rebound, then dashes to shoot in his or her own court before the other team can catch up.

field goal: a successful basket made while the game clock is running, worth two or three points.

five-second violation: after taking possession of the ball, an out-of-bounds player has five seconds to pass the ball in-bounds.

flagrant foul: nasty, unsportsmanlike behavior during a game that involves bodily contact between players, such as kicking, hitting, or elbowing.

forward: most teams have two forwards on court at once. On offense, forwards shoot the ball and help the center. On defense, forwards go after rebounds.

foul: see **flagrant foul, personal foul,** and **technical foul.**

foul out: when a professional player acquires his or her sixth foul in a game, he or she is not allowed to play for the rest of that game. A player close to fouling out is in "foul trouble."

frontcourt: the side of the court where the offense can score. The offense may not take the ball from its frontcourt to its backcourt. Once a team acquires the ball, it has ten seconds to get the ball to its frontcourt. Referring to players, the frontcourt is the center and forwards.

goaltending: also called basket interference. A player may not block an opponent's shot if the ball is in the air directly over the basket and on the way down.

guard: a team usually has two guards. Often called ball handlers, guards sometimes don't shoot as much as centers or forwards. Instead, guards on offense help move the ball to the frontcourt by passing and dribbling. On defense, guards try to stop the offense.

hang time: the time a player spends in the air while attempting a jump shot, dunk, or layup.

held ball: when one offensive and one defensive player grasp the ball at the same time. The referee calls for a jump ball to decide who gets it. (See **jump ball.**)

hook shot: the player with the ball has his or her back to the basket. He or she jumps, turns in midair, and arcs the ball over his or her head with one hand for the basket.

in-bounds pass: when a player out-of-bounds passes the ball to a teammate who is in-bounds. Players pass from this area after the other team fouls or makes a basket. The passer may move side to side during an in-bounds pass after a basket. After a foul, the passer must stand and pass.

jump ball: after a held ball occurs, a referee tosses the ball straight up. One player from each team tries to tip the ball to his or her team.

jump shot: a player jumps in the air and shoots.

key: the foul lane and the free throw circle used to form a keylike shape. That's why this area was called the key, a name still used even now that the lane has been widened.

lane: Also called "paint." When a player is "in the lane," he or she is in the rectangle formed by the free-throw line, the out-of-bounds line, and the lines even with the backboard.

lane violation: when a player moves into the lane for a rebound before the ball leaves the free-throw shooter's hand.

man-to-man: when defensive players guard a particular person on the other team.

net: the woven ropes attached to the basket's rim.

offense: the team with the ball trying to score.

overtime: if a game is tied after four quarters, an extra period of five minutes is added. A game tied at the end of an overtime will add overtimes until a period ends with a winner.

palming: a violation. (See **carrying**.)

personal foul: illegal contact with an opponent.

pick: When an offensive player helps a teammate who has the ball by keeping an opponent away. Often said "set a pick." Also: to legally hinder an opponent's movement. (See **screen**.)

pick-and-roll: After getting in an opponent's way, an offensive player quickly moves away, or "rolls," closer to the basket to receive a pass and shoot. (See **pick**.)

pivot: 1. changing directions with one foot while keeping the other foot on the floor. 2. the part of the court near the basket.

point guard: the guard who handles the ball most and directs offensive players on the court.

post: near the basket but outside the lane. (See **lane**.)

post up: when an offensive player with the ball is facing away from the basket before turning to shoot over or around the defender.

power forward: often the bigger of a team's two forwards. Power forwards rebound and score.

quadruple-double: when, during one game, a player reaches double figures (10 or more) in four of the following categories: points, rebounds, assists, steals, or blocked shots.

rebound: when a ball doesn't go through the basket but bounces away, and somebody grabs it. If the shooter or the shooter's teammate grabs the ball, it's called an offensive rebound. If an opponent gets it, that's a defensive rebound.

rejection: a blocked shot.

screen: See **pick**.

set shot: when a player shoots with both feet on the floor.

shot clock: a clock that counts down a set number of seconds. If a team does not try to shoot the ball within a limited amount of time, the ball will be turned over to the other team.

sideline: the long side boundaries of the court.

sixth man: a multitalented player who is not a starter. The sixth man is usually the first substitute the coach calls off the bench when a starter takes a break or leaves the game.

steal: to take the ball away from the opposing team by intercepting a pass or a dribble.

technical foul: a foul that does not involve contact with an opponent. Breaking game rules, calling too many time outs, or behaving like a poor sport are all technical fouls.

three-second rule: no part of an offensive player's body may be in the free-throw lane for longer than three seconds during play.

timeline: the line dividing the two teams' courts. Also called the ten-second line. The timeline got its name because a team must cross the line to its own side within ten seconds after getting the ball. (See **frontcourt.**)

tip-in: to reach up and tip a missed shot back into the basket.

tip-off: to start each game, the referee puts up a jump ball to decide who gets the ball. See (**jump ball.**)

transition: to shift from offense to defense, or defense to offense, when the ball moves from one end of the court to the other.

travel: a violation that can only be committed by the player with the ball. This player may not drag one foot, move more than two steps without dribbling, or jump and land without passing or shooting.

triple-double: when a player achieves double digits (10 or more) in three of five categories: scoring, assists, rebounds, steals, and blocked shots.

turnover: when the offensive team loses the ball.

violation: when a team member breaks a rule (commits a violation), that team loses possession of the ball. A violation does not count as a personal foul.

wing: the part of the court on each side of the free-throw line, outside the three-point area.

zone defense: when defensive players stay on an assigned part of the court, guarding opponents who come into that area. Illegal in the NBA.

For More Information

Books

Goodman, Michael. *Boston Celtics*. Mankato, Minn.: Creative Education, Inc., 1998.

Klinzing, Jim and Mike Klinzing. *Fundamental Basketball*. Minneapolis: Lerner, 1996.

MacDonald, Frank. *Golden State Warriors*. Mankato, Minn.: Creative Education, 1984.

Mayers, Florence Cassen. *The NBA Alphabet*. New York: Abrams Publishers, 1996.

Moore, Jim. *Washington Bullets*. Mankato, Minn.: Creative Education, Inc., 1984.

Vancil, Mark. *NBA Basketball Basics*. New York: Sterling Publishing Co., 1995.

Vancil, Mark. *NBA Basketball Offense Basics*. New York: Sterling Publishing Co., 1996.

Books for Older Readers

Hession, Joseph. *Lakers: Collectors Edition*. San Francisco: Foghorn Press, Inc., 1994.

The Official NBA Basketball Encyclopedia, second edition. Edited by Alex Sachare. New York: Villard Books, 1994.

Phelps, Richard "Digger" with John Walters. *Basketball for Dummies*. Foster City, Calif.: IDG Books, 1997.

Pluto, Terry. *Tall Tales*. New York: Simon and Schuster, 1992.

Internet Resources

www.nba.com
The official league Web site is packed with information.

www.wnba.com
NBA fans wanting to follow the "sister" league should start here.

www.ableague.com
The WNBA's rival, the American Basketball League, isn't seen on TV a lot. However, all their news awaits at this site.

www.hoophall.com
The Basketball Hall of Fame is closer than you think.

INDEX

Page numbers in *italics* refer to illustrations.

Abdul-Jabbar, Kareem, 23–24, 27, 33, 42
Alford, Steve, 34
Armstrong, B.J., 40
Atlanta Hawks, 36
Auerbach, Arnold "Red," 14–15, *15*, 20, 39, 40

Barkley, Charles, 28
Barksdale, Don, 33
Barnett, Dick, 41
Barry, Rick, 30–31, 45
Baylor, Elgin, 27
Bird, Larry, 16–18, *17*, 26
Bol, Manute, 24–25
Boston Celtics, 14, 15, 20, *21*, *23*, 25, 26, *32*, 39, 40, 47
Bowie, Sam, 40

Carr, Antoine, 53
Cartwright, Bill, 6
Castellani, John, 27
Chamberlain, Wilt, 22–23, *23*, 27
Chicago Bulls, 5, 6, 8–12, 18, 27, 35, *36*, 40–41, 48, *49*, 51, *52*, 53, 55
Chicago White Sox, 12
Cousy, Bob, 33
Cowens, Dave, 25
Cunningham, Billy, 13

Daly, Chuck, 13–14, *14*
Drexler, Clyde "The Glide," 40

English, Alex, 29
Erving, Julius "Dr. J," 26, *27*, 38

Gottlieb, Eddie, 22

Grant, Horace, 6

Hansen, Bobby, 40
Harter, Dick, 17
Havlicek, John, 39–41, *47*, 47
Hill, Grant, 26
Hodges, Craig, 44
Hornacek, Jeff, 51
Houston Rockets, 25, *34*

Indiana Pacers, 16, *17*, 37

Jackson, Phil, 6, 8, *8*, 9, 18, 40–41
Johnson, Earvin "Magic," 5–6, *7*, 8–11, 33–34, 42
Jones, Bobby, 38, 39, *39*
Jones, Sam, 47
Jordan, Michael, 5, 6, 7, 8–12, 18, 27, 35, *36*, 37, 40, 45, 48, *49*, 50, *52*, 53, 55

Keefe, Adam, 51
Kerr, Steve, 51
King, Stacey, 40
Krause, Jerry, 12
Kukoc, Toni, 13, 41, 50

Longley, Luc, 50
Los Angeles Clippers, 39
Los Angeles Lakers, 5–6, 9, 10, 27, 33–35, 39, 41

Malone, Karl, 28, 48, 50, 51, *52*, 53
Malone, Moses, 38
Maravich, "Pistol" Pete, 46
McAdoo, Bob, 41–42
McHale, Kevin, 39

•63•

Miami Heat, 37
Mikan, George, 20, 22
Miller, Cheryl, 37
Miller, Reggie, 37
Milwaukee Bucks, 23
Minneapolis Lakers, 20
Motta, Dick, 16
Murphy, Calvin, 45–46

Naismith, James, 46
New York Knicks, 22, 27, 35

Olajuwon, Hakeem, 25
O'Neal, Shaquille, 35, 44, *45*

Parish, Robert, 39
Paxson, Jim, 40
Paxson, John, 6
Payton, Gary, 33
Perkins, Sam, 9
Pettit, Bob, 28, *29*
Philadelphia 76ers, 22, 26, *32*, 38–39, 47
Philadelphia Warriors, 22, *23*
Pippen, Scottie, 6, 9, *10*, 10, 27, 40, 48, *49*, 50, 51, 53, 55
Portland Trailblazers, 40–41
Price, Brent, *34*

Ramsey, Frank, 39, *40*

Reinsdorf, Jerry, 12
Riley, Pat, 16
Rodman, Dennis "Worm," 28, 38
Russell, Bill, *15*, 15–16, 20–22, *21*, *23*

St. Louis Hawks, 28, *29*
Sampson, Ralph, 25
Seattle SuperSonics, 16
Skiles, Scott, 34
Smith, Steve, *36*, 37
Starks, John, 35
Stockton, John, 33–34, 46, 48, *49*, 50, 51
Stokes, Carl, 53

Thurmond, Nate, 24, 25
Twyman, Jack, 15, 35, 43, 53

Unseld, Wes, 25
Utah Jazz, 33, 48, *49*, 50, 51, *52*, 53, 55

Walton, Bill, 39
Washington Bullets, 24
West, Jerry, 34–35
Westhead, Paul, 6
Wilkens, Lenny, 35
Wilkins, Dominique, 29–30
Williams, Herb, 51
Williams, Scott, 40
Winter, Fred "Tex," 18, 50